Marie-Louise Fitzpatrick is an award-winning Irish author-illustrator, whose books *Izzy and Skunk* and *You, Me and the Deep Blue Sea* have both won the Bisto Book of the Year award. Her warm and distinctive style has attracted fans from all over the world. Beth, the heroine of *Silly School*, is based on Marie-Louise's own niece. You can read more about Beth's adventures in Marie-Louise's first book for Frances Lincoln, *Silly Mummy, Silly Daddy*, which was shortlisted for the Irish Children's Book of the Year.

For Siobhán, love M-L.F.

Silly School copyright © Frances Lincoln Limited 2007
Text and illustrations copyright © Marie-Louise Fitzpatrick 2007

First published in Great Britain and the USA in 2007 by
Frances Lincoln Children's Books, 4 Torriano Mews,
Torriano Avenue, London NW5 2RZ
www.franceslincoln.com

First paperback edition published in Great Britain in 2008

British Library Cataloguing in Publication Data available on request

ISBN 978-1-84507-589-7

Illustrated with gouache

Printed in China

1 3 5 7 9 8 6 4 2

Silly School

Marie-Louise Fitzpatrick

FRANCES LINCOLN
CHILDREN'S BOOKS

Today is Beth's first day
at school.

"Let's go, Bethy-Boo,"
says Mummy.

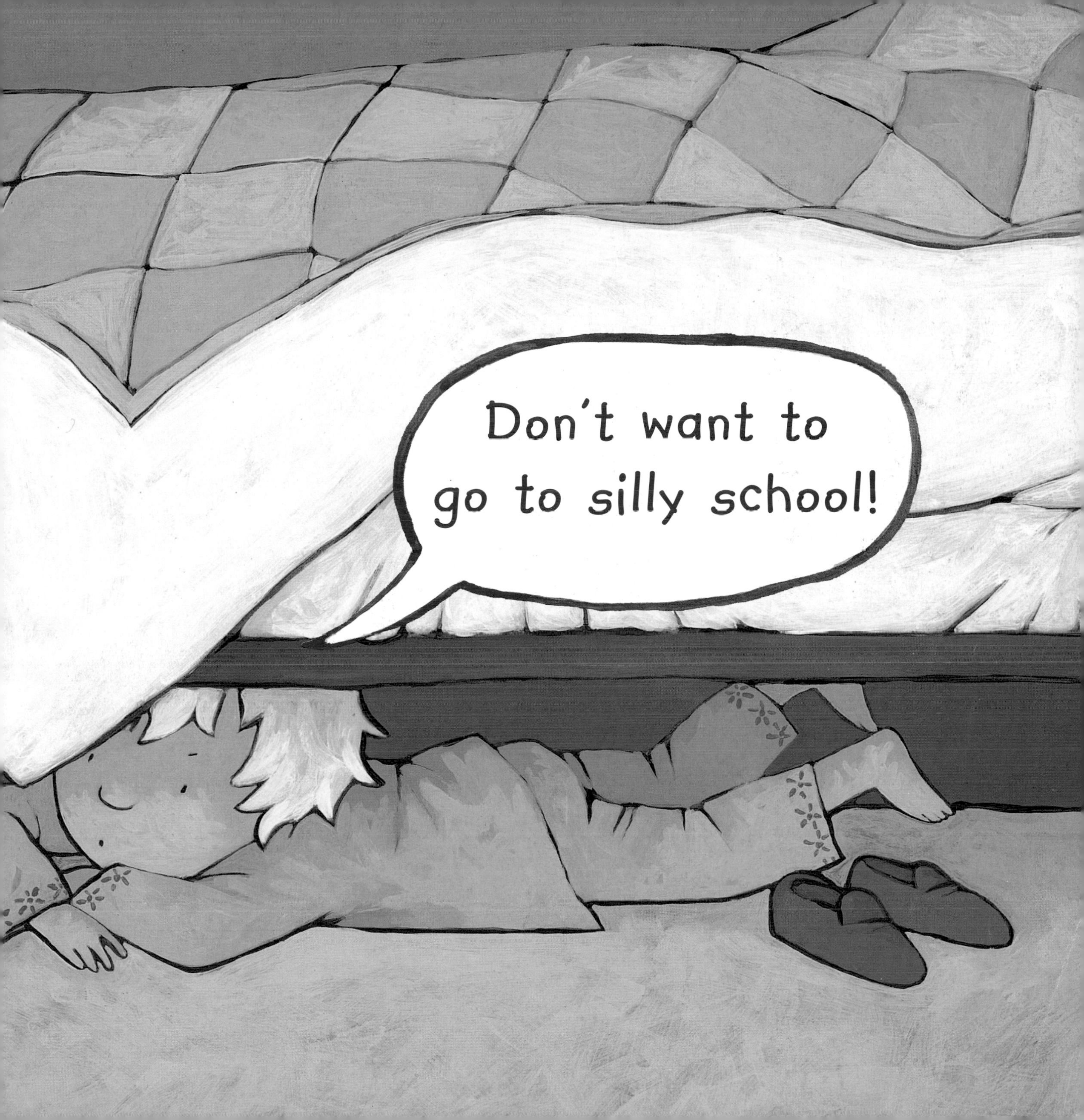
Don't want to go to silly school!

"There'll be singing," says Aunty Bea. "La, la, la, laaaa!"

"There'll be toys," says Ann.
"Cuddly-wuddly toys."

Don't want to go!

"Painting," says Aunty Mel.
"Splish, splash, splosh!"

"Games," says Grandad.
"Ready, steady, go!"

"Lunchtimes and storytimes," say Uncle Ben and Gran.

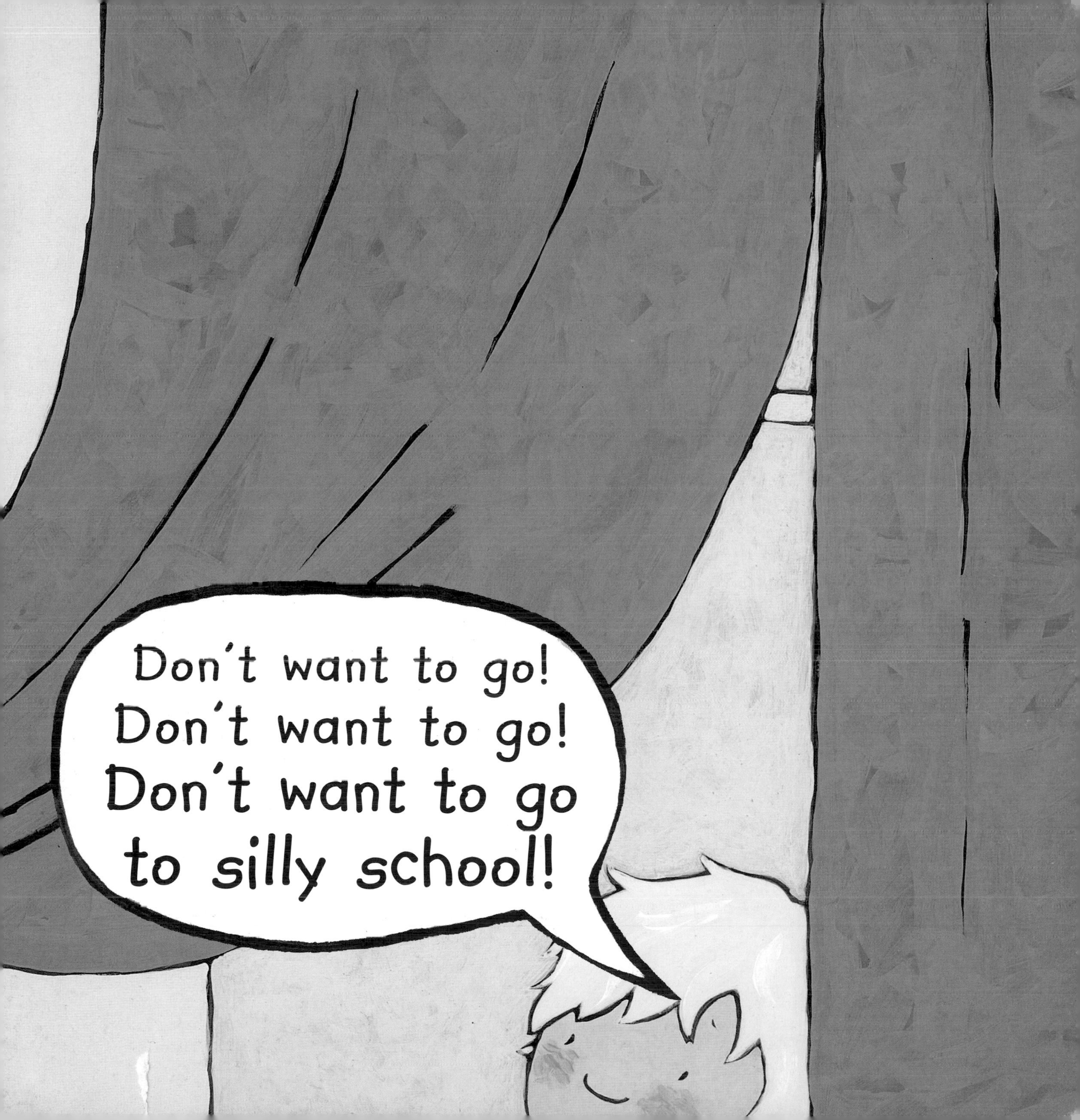
Don't want to go! Don't want to go! Don't want to go to silly school!

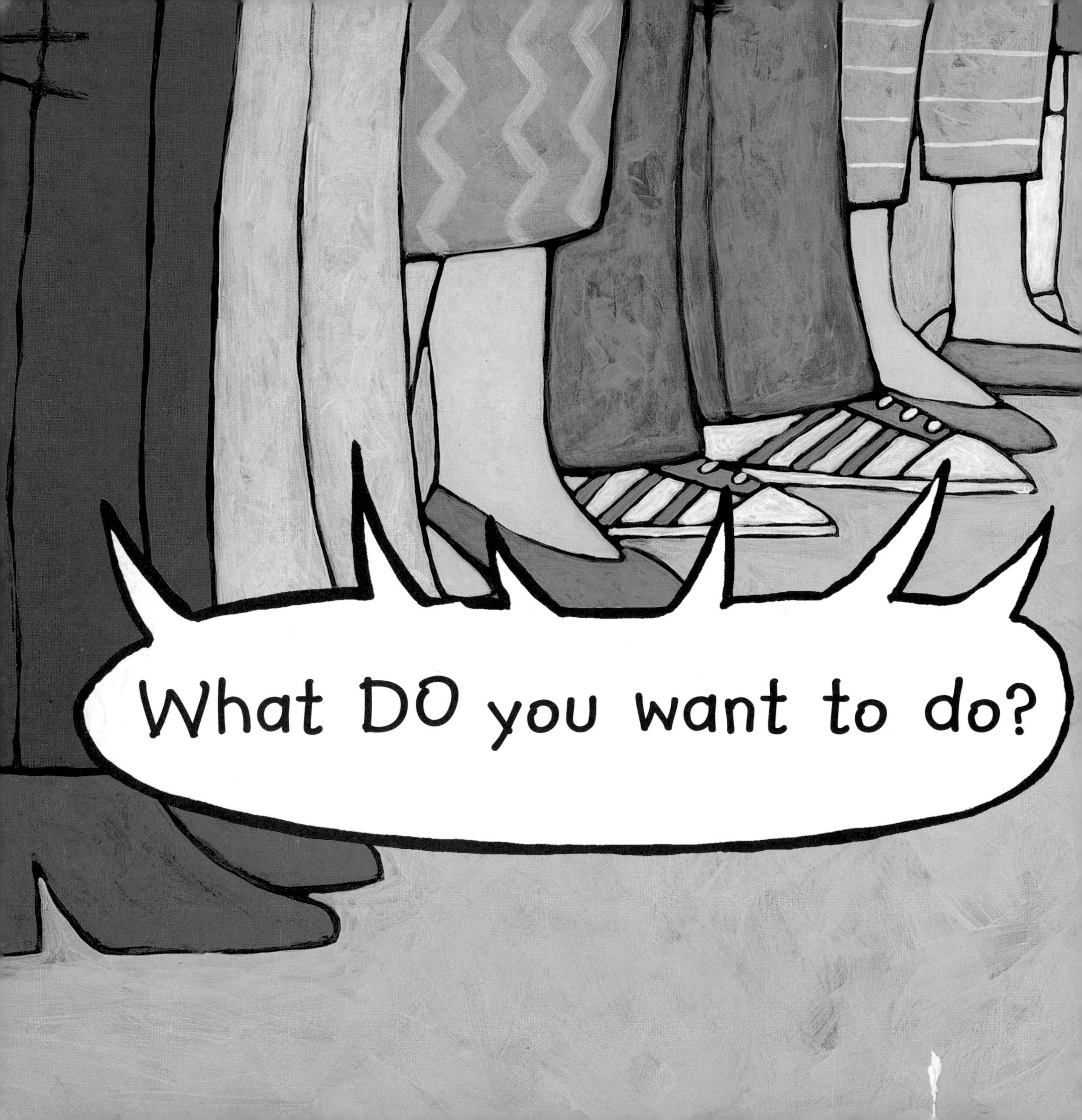
What DO you want to do?

"But your friends are all at school," says Daddy.

School's over.
It's home-time.
Here comes Daddy.

MORE TITLES FROM
FRANCES LINCOLN CHILDREN'S BOOKS

Silly Mummy, Silly Daddy (UK)
Silly Mommy, Silly Daddy (US)

Beth is VERY cross today and will not smile –
not even a little bit! The whole family tries to put
her in a sunny mood but they are just SILLY!
Can Clever Big Sister save the day?

ISBN 978-1-84507-592-7 (UK)
ISBN 978-1-84507-547-7 (US)

I Have Feelings
Jana Novotny Hunter
Illustrated by Sue Porter

Everybody has feelings – especially me and you!
Waking up is my best time – then I feel happy.
And when we go to the park I feel really excited.
But when my baby sister gets first turn on the swing,
I start feeling jealous!

ISBN 978-0-7112-1734-8 (UK)

I Can Do It!
Jana Novotny Hunter
Illustrated by Lucy Richards

Little Guinea Pig can do all sorts of things!
He can pound his playdough, use his paws to scribble
in the sand and bang his drum when he wants to be LOUD!

ISBN 978-1-84507-586-6

Frances Lincoln titles are available from all good bookshops.
You can also buy books and find out more about your favourite titles,
authors and illustrators on our website: www.franceslincoln.com